ANIMAL VS. ANIMAL

WHO'S THE FASTEST?

BY KIRSTY HOLMES

Please visit our website, www.garethstevens.com. For a free color catalog of all our high-quality books, call toll free 1-800-542-2595 or fax 1-877-542-2596.

Cataloging-in-Publication Data

Names: Holmes, Kirsty.
Title: Who's the fastest? / Kirsty Holmes.
Description: New York : Gareth Stevens Publishing, 2022. | Series: Animal vs. animal | Includes glossary and index.
Identifiers: ISBN 9781534537583 (pbk.) | ISBN 9781534537606 (library bound) | ISBN 9781534537590 (6 pack) | ISBN 9781534537613 (ebook)
Subjects: LCSH: Animal locomotion--Juvenile literature. | Animal mechanics--Juvenile literature.
Classification: LCC QP301.H68 2022 | DDC 591.5'7--dc23

Published in 2022 by
Gareth Stevens Publishing
29 East 21st Street
New York, NY 10010

© 2022 Booklife Publishing
This edition is published by arrangement with Booklife Publishing

Edited by: Robin Twiddy
Designed by: Danielle Rippengill

All rights reserved. No part of this book may be reproduced in any form without permission in writing from the publisher, except by a reviewer.

Printed in the United States of America

Some of the images in this book illustrate individuals who are models. The depictions do not imply actual situations or events.

CPSIA compliance information: Batch #CSGS22: For further information contact Gareth Stevens, New York, New York at 1-800-542-2595.

Find us on  

IMAGE CREDITS

All images are courtesy of Shutterstock.com, unless otherwise specified. With thanks to Getty Images, Thinkstock Photo, and iStockphoto. Cover – Ovocheva, Stepova Oksana, Abscent. Images used on every page – Ovocheva, Stepova Oksana. 2 – Maquiladora. 5 – ONYXprj, Abscent. 6&7 – Guingm. 7 – Maquiladora. 8 – Sudhir Misra. 9 – Mathias Podstawka. 8&9 – Guingm. 10&11 – Abscent. 12 – By Roland Speck (White-throated needletail (Hirundapus caudacutus)) via Wikimedia Commons. 13 – Elliotte Rusty Harold. 12&13 – Guingm. 14&15 – Abscent. 16 – kelldallfall. 17 – stockphoto mania. 16&17 – Maquiladora, Guingm. 18&19 – Maquiladora, Abscent. 20&21 – amiloslava. 22 – Guingm. 23 – Abscent.

CONTENTS

Words that look like this can be found in the glossary on page 24.

THE GREAT AND SMALL GAMES

Come one, come all!

It's the Great and Small Games!

See nature's speediest creatures in action!

Today's events:

Catch Me if You Can!

Capture the Flag!

Race Around the Reef!

These events will quickly decide once and for all:

Who's the Fastest?

Welcome, welcome, one and all,
to games where creatures GREAT and SMALL
can come together, ready to race
and see which creatures take first place.
TODAY'S EVENTS will prove, at last,
just what it means to be called "fast."
And so, without much more ado,
this RACCOON referee brings you...

THE CONTENDERS

Let's find out some facts and figures about today's contenders!

Needletail Swift
Swift by Name, Swift by Nature
Wingspan: Up to 15 inches (38 cm)
Weight: About 1 ounce (32 g)
Speed: Up to 105 miles per hour (170 kph)

Peregrine Falcon
The Daredevil Diver
Wingspan: 4 feet (1.2 m)
Weight: Up to 1.8 pounds (0.8 kg)
Speed: About 200 miles per hour (320 kph)

Antelope
Supersonic Springbok
Height: Up to 2.6 feet (0.8 m)
Weight: About 90 pounds (41 kg)
Speed: Up to 55 miles per hour (88 kph)

Cheetah
The Quick Kitty
Height: Up to 3 feet (0.9 m)
Weight: Up to 160 pounds (73 kg)
Speed: Up to 65 miles per hour (105 kph)
Sailfish
The Rapid Rock Star
Length: Up to 10 feet (3 m)
Weight: 880 pounds (400 kg)
Speed: Up to 68 miles per hour (109 kph)
Black Marlin
Ninja of the Seas
Length: Up to 15 feet (4.5 m)
Weight: Up to 1,650 pounds (748 kg)
Speed: Up to 50 miles per hour (80 kph)

SPRINGBOK

Jumping into action, our first contender is the springbok. He's an amazing antelope who can jump distances of 13 feet (4 m) and outrun most **predators**. This horned **herbivore** usually travels in packs – but he'll be running solo today!

Nickname:
The Supersonic Springbok

Super Speed:
Springboks can jump up to 13 feet (4 m) – this is called pronking!

VS. CHEETAH

He's fierce! He's fast! He's fur-ocious! From sub-Saharan Africa, this **carnivore** kitty can't climb trees, but who cares when you're this quick!

Nickname:
The Quick Kitty

Super Speed:
Cheetahs can reach their top speed in just three seconds!

Cheetahs are the only big cats that can't roar!

MEOW!

CATCH ME IF YOU CAN

To decide which of these African animals is the fastest, it's a straight race across the **savanna**! On your mark... Get set... GO!

Both of these mega mammals are very fast, but the cheetah is 10 miles per hour (16 kph) faster!

NEEDLETAIL SWIFT VS.

TWEET! TWEET!

This fast flapper spends most of its life in the air, only coming to the ground to **nest**. With so much flight time, it's no wonder this feathered friend is so speedy!

Nickname:
Swift by Name, Swift by Nature

Super Speed:
The needletail swift has a very **sleek** body. This helps air easily pass over it.

PEREGRINE FALCON

Swooping in from, well, everywhere on Earth (except Antarctica), this rapid **raptor** is also known as the duck hawk, as its favorite food is duck! Keep your eyes on the skies, as this bird of prey is a diver!

Nickname:
The Daredevil Diver

Super Speed:
The peregrine falcon's heart can beat up to 900 times per minute! This helps it fly fast.

SQWARK!

This bird can catch prey mid-flight!

CAPTURE THE FLAG

It's a race for the skies as two of the world's fastest birds fly for the flag. The first to capture the flag wins! Ready... Set... FLY!

The swift can even sleep while flying!

Swift Statistics

Horizontal flight speed: 105 mph

The needletail swift is very fast in flapping flight, but nothing can beat the falcon's dive! It's the fastest animal anywhere on Earth!

Falcon Statistics

Vertical dive speed: 200 mph

That's almost twice as fast!

Round two goes to the **peregrine falcon!**

BLACK MARLIN

This pointy-faced fish from the Pacific chases down squid, tuna, and mackerel, so she has to be fast! She comes to the surface during the full moon, and when she's excited she gets bright blue stripes!

Nickname:
Ninja of the Seas

Super Strength:
It is believed that the marlin's long bill helps it glide through the water.

VS. SAILFISH

The marlin's colorful cousin is easy to spot – he's got a huge sail on his back, and changes colors when he's excited! He's an **apex predator** with a funky attitude and a giant jump!

Nickname:
The Rapid Rock Star

Super Strength:
The sailfish has a moon-shaped tail that acts like the wings of a bird, helping it swim fast!

Sailfish have razor-sharp bills!

BRING IT ON!

RACE AROUND THE REEF

Two fast fish. One round reef. Who will be the fastest in the timed **laps**? There's only one way to find out!

First up: the black marlin. Three... Two... One... SWIM!

The black marlin is about 40 times faster than the average human swimmer!

Black Marlin

Speed: 50 mph

Time: 00:00:45

The black marlin made it around our reef track in 45 seconds! Can the sailfish beat her time? Three... Two... One... SWIM!

HALL OF FAME

Pronghorn Antelope
Relative of the springbok.

Length: Around 4.5 feet (1.4 m)

Weight: Around 110 pounds (50 kg)

Speed: Around 60 mph (96 kph)

Blue Wildebeest
African herbivore hunted by lions.

Height: Up to 8 feet (2.4 m) at shoulder

Weight: 640 pounds (290 kg)

Speed: Around 50 mph (80 kph)

Brown Hare
Always ready to outrun its predators.

Length: 2.6 feet (0.8 m) including tail

Weight: Up to 11 pounds (5 kg)

Speed: Up to 44 mph (70 kph)

Lion
Big cat from sub-Saharan Africa.

Height: 4 feet (1.2 m) at shoulder

Weight: Up to 550 pounds (250 kg)

Speed: Up to 50 mph (80 kph)

You've seen which beasts are incredibly strong;
now take our quiz – it won't take you long!

Questions

1. How quickly can a cheetah reach top speed?
2. What is "pronking"?
3. What is another name for a peregrine falcon?
4. What is a needletail swift's top speed in horizontal flight?
5. What do black marlin like to eat?
6. What happens to a sailfish when it gets excited?

ACTIVITY

Practice makes perfect when it comes to speed. Running, swimming, or on your bike...

...getting faster is what we like!

Answers from page 22: 1. 3 seconds. 2. When a springbok jumps straight up. 3. Duck hawk. 4. 105 mph. 5. Squid, tuna, and mackerel. 6. It changes color.

GLOSSARY

apex predator	an animal that is at the top of the food chain and is not prey for another animal
carnivore	an animal that only eats meat
herbivore	an animal that only eats plants
horizontal	running along the ground from left to right
lap	a complete trip around a marked track
nest	to build a nest and raise young
predator	an animal that hunts other animals for food
raptor	a bird of prey; a bird that feeds on animals or other birds
savanna	flat grassland found mostly in Africa
sleek	shiny or smooth
vertical	straight up and down
wingspan	the distance between the tips of a bird's wings

INDEX